CHRISTMAS SPIRIT

Meredith Carson, World Codex Staff

The World Codex, LLC © 2018

Contents

INTRODUCTION

"Are you looking for a short story to recite during a Christmas party or perform as a short play? Look no further. The World Codex Staff and Meredith Carson have written a great tale with dramatic potential in the short story, Christmas Spirit. Written in the believable voice of Ebenezer Scrooge, this captivating twist on Dickens' A Christmas Carol is sure to create a new Christmas tradition in many homes, drama clubs, and schools.

Meredith Carson unfolds the "Christmas Spirit" in a well-written, fast-paced, and delightful narrative. We readers and listeners alike sit back and let our imaginations fly. This page-turner keeps us wanting more. We cannot wait to find out what happens next. In fact, you may think you know where the story is leading just before you learn that you do not. In Christmas Spirit, we allow Meredith Carson to spirit us away from our everyday life and drop us back in time to our days of sipping hot chocolate while our moms read us special stories at Christmas time, and this is a special Christmas story. It is intriguing, exciting, and heartbreaking. All three make for a retold Christmas story year after year.

I love the narrative voice of Ebenezer Scrooge. The drama is wonderful and enchanting. I can easily see Christmas Spirit performed at parties and on the stage. Meredith Carson has written a story that will become a Christmas tradition in our homes and in our hearts. This short Christmas story deserves a five star rating."

~ Geree McDermott for Readers' Favorite ~

CHRISTMAS SPIRIT

"Humans are amphibians - half spirit and half animal. As spirits they belong to the eternal world, but as animals they inhabit time." ~ C.S. Lewis

On a bleak and wretched December night in the City of London, I quietly passed through a vacuous void. While the pendulum's swinging grew ever slower, the hands on the old grandfather clock stopped moving forward. It was at that moment I realized that I was exiting this world and entering the ethereal realm. Shuffling off my mortal coil as it were, I eventually succumbed to the stark reality that my death was now a cold hard fact. I discovered that to be true in an instant because I could see my poor lifeless corpse bundled below me, lying prostrate in my sleeping chamber.

The next thing I became aware of was that I had arrived in this domain from which I am speaking to you presently. I came without fanfare and not during any heroic act, but from my ever-weakening condition which was brought on from so many years of poor diet. As many of you may not be aware, I suffered from a case of chronic cough and deadly consumption. Had I known better I would have improved the quality of my fare in my earlier years. I have not dined on a morsel of delight for nearly two centuries, yet the flavors I imagine are sensed and savored at the mere thought of my desire for such. Since the night I heard the ticking of the clock cease, my sensory perception has been surreal at best. I've come to understand better the meaning of the German phrase - Zeit ist eine illusion - time is an illusion.

More and more curious eyes and ears are witnessing the sordid and morbid tale of how I engaged my energies while I lived and worked among others just like yourselves. Perhaps the waking world with its wondering eyes may not have considered what became of me since my story, my life, came to its unrecorded inglorious conclusion so long ago. I have returned now to erase several inconsistencies about my character forever, so to speak, and to make recompense for the debt that was once paid on my behalf. I admit that I deserved no such favor, and because of that my conscience has plagued me for far too long. My presence here is but for a very short time, for I've come just once more to tickle your ears through this magical medium. I will attempt to present my case at this crucial precipice and pivotal crossroad in your history to the best of my ability. I feel it is my duty to appear to you this way to deliver a foreshadowing of things to come, for both clarity and posterity.

I have been chosen, just as I previously was, yet this time not merely as a man but as a spectre. I am burdened with the task of finishing what was conceived millennia before my own story even began - before my own incarnation ever existed. I am the ghost who visits you now in your homes while you conduct the business of the living. Pause now if you will to consider your vocation, inspiration, and motivation - because all that you do and why it is done is a matter of great importance.

I impose upon you now wherever you may be, just as I was once so similarly accosted, not out of malice but from a place of humility for having been the scoundrel that I once was so long ago. As such, I offer you a brief glimpse, the opportunity to peer through my eyes which have become windows into the realm where I now dwell in repose and contemplation. The entirety of humankind, each and every soul, must soon prepare to follow me and enter here. Not far from my grave there is a headstone inscribed with the words offered in memory of a young woman who died far too early in life; her name is Elizabeth. This is what it says on her gravestone:

REMEMBER ME AS YOU PASS BY -

AS YOU ARE NOW - SO ONCE WAS I

AS I AM NOW - YOU SOON MUST BE,

PREPARE FOR DEATH, TO FOLLOW ME...

Let me properly introduce myself for those of you who may be wondering who I am, my name is Ebenezer Scrooge. More to the point, I am the apparition who was once the greedy miser so miraculously saved from his own self-induced torment by four benevolent spirits. My partner, Jacob Marley, vehemently lifted the veil of my selfish enterprises which so effectively blinded me for far too long a period in my life. The miserable manifestation was first and foremost the spectre of despair and horror which opened my eyes, against my will, yet to my great benefit. Warned was I with a subdued benevolence by a dark manner of his own device, to the great perils ahead which I could not yet see. A future that may have only been avoided while I was still on earth alive and able to choose, just as all of you are now, and to his great credit, Marley shocked me out of my waking slumber and into my purpose for being alive.

Poor Marley, who no longer wanders the earth in the chains of his misery, has passed on into the infinite forever. For he served so well what he deemed a meaningless life - through his unwitting sacrifice - and now exists on a diminished plane far beyond the reach of my eyes and sound of my voice. Never again shall our paths meet. For even now when I call out his name in hopes of rekindling our friendship for old time's sake, there is only silence - deflating, deafening and frightful - as though that same void I passed through the night I died exists now between us. No spirit has the power to breach that vacuous void once their path has been decided.

On the freezing winter's night that I left my bed for the last time, I was trapped within a feverish dream, wrapped like an infant, blanket upon blanket. I envisioned myself wandering amidst a vast ethereal plane as a spirit, no longer flesh, and bone. Time was of no import, and distance was beyond any means of my measure. I was yet unaware that my dream was the process of my body leaving this world. Hence, I had crossed over and had become a creature no different from those who had visited me years before during that fateful Christmas Eve. Where, in the short span of just that one night, I was no longer transfixed by the desire to better myself at the expense of those less fortunate than I. My transformation from the darkness of avarice and into the light of mirth became my joy and my vocation, as many millions of you already know. What you do not yet know is what I experienced years later when my time on earth had ended. That is the substance of things not yet seen - nor fully grasped - yet inevitable and magnificent.

Inside of my transitory dream, visions seeped into my mind and have left their enduring mark on my awareness, and more importantly my conscience. My bizarre and transformative trek across this plane of existence I have never shared with a single living soul until this Christmas season. The time has come to bequeath to you all everything that I have seen. Those impressions of your world and your possible future of which I am now aware, and the shocking end of the 3rd millennium as you know it to be. First, however, I'd like to take you back to my past where my own Christmas story indeed began, as an ordinary child. Come with me now to a time long lost, yet ever so vivid in my memories. When I was just a boy these things shaped my world. Although then, much to my dismay, I was unaware of their depth, breadth, and indiscernible consequences.

I've never had reason to relive this experience from my past and to be truthful I hesitate to do it now because of the harsh memory it still pains me to conjure. Alas, at the time I was visited by those three transportive spirits on Christmas Eve, I had done my best to all but forget what I had witnessed so many years ago. I shall relive it in the telling just this one last time. Much to my surprise, the ghost of my Christmas past never brought it to light during our short time together. I suppose that it may have been because he could see ahead to this exact moment, knowing all the while that I would share it when the time became paramount.

I do so believe that the faith and perseverance of a child is a dominant force in the universe. It seems clear to me that I am here expressing these thoughts as perhaps a beacon of hope to help illuminate an often all too dark and dreary world, as was once done so graciously for me. To that end, I take you back in time to the story that started it all. This event shaped me into the man that I once was, and the spirit I have become. It begins with these few harsh words which my father said to me one painfully unforgettable Christmas Eve Day.

"Before I give you my permission to frolic in the snow with your friend, you will obey my wishes. You will tidy your room and make your bed just as mother has told you to do several times already."

"I will father, and then I will go and get that turkey I saw yesterday for Christmas dinner tomorrow."

"Humbug boy! You will come back wet, cold and empty-handed, mark my words."

A few minutes later, I took the opportunity to plead my case to my mother after my father had left on a venture that was kept secret from my sister and me. Although I wish she had made me stay with her that day and obey my father, this is what transpired. Foolishly, I attempted to disarm her with my subtle, disappointed frown which seemed to always get the job done.

"Mother, it is the day before Christmas, and yesterday I saw a big turkey in the hedgerow just a stone's throw away from the Miller's farm. Peter and I chased him but could not catch him. Please let me go with his father to hunt a Christmas goose, or perhaps that fat gobbler."

"Wicked boy, you possess mysterious means of softening my heart, though you bring my resolve to a boil at times. Go, go have your fun! I will do your dirty work for you, but this is the only present for Christmas you shall connive from me this day. Be off with you now!"

That was the last convivial conversation I had with my mother that day. Without any further ado, I donned my winter coat, hat, and mittens, and I was off in a hurry to catch up to the other members of our hunting party. They had left but a quarter of an hour before me, and I knew where they were heading. Their footprints in the freshly fallen snow provided a neat and precise trail to follow, and it made the chase all the more fun for me.

When I finally caught up to the both of them, they had just arrived at Parker's pond. I remember how the snow had covered the little lake in a blanket of white, making it almost entirely invisible and equally as treacherous. Much to my surprise when I got closer I was astonished to see that it was not Peter, but his sister Elizabeth who had joined her father for the hunt on that Christmas Eve Day.

"Where's Peter?" My curiosity was peaked, and I was a bit concerned.

"Peter is sick in his bed. He has a fever from playing outside and getting soaking wet yesterday."

His father seemed a bit upset because Peter had spent the day with me, but I just kept quiet.

The previous year, there was only Peter and his father together on the hunt, but I was the first person to hear that Peter had received a silver coin as his reward for spotting the coveted Christmas bird. With a good measure of remuneration, his father had made their escapade together more fun and rewarding as well, as he was a good father. Elizabeth wanted to be the one to try and win the prize for herself in the absence of her little brother. She too desired the coveted silver crown for her efforts. It would have been the Christmas money spent on a gift for her kind and gentle mother, but that was never to be. Both Elizabeth and I were equally determined to succeed in our quest, Elizabeth, however, in her overzealousness, had impetuously thrown caution to the wind.

Just as we had hoped, not more than a few minutes after our arrival there, the serendipitous sound of a small flock of Canadian geese returning to their home grew louder in our eager ears. They were unaware that their watery world had frozen over early, and the momentarily perplexed birds circled the lake providing Mr. Miller ample time to choose his target carefully.

It had begun snowing lightly which made it hard for me to look upward into the grey sky without blinking. The snowy scene was picturesque and serene until Mr. Miller fired his rifle. The thunderous shot hit its mark, and the lifeless goose plummeted earthward. As I was absorbing the experience in my contemplative state, I failed to react except to jump a bit from the loud jolting sound of the gun. Elizabeth, however, had taken off running to retrieve her prize before I could respond to what had happened.

The chain of events that cascaded out of control because of that one single shot still strikes fear into my being. Elizabeth had forgotten all about the invisible lake, and as the goose was falling upon its frozen surface, she ran as fast as she could to fetch it. It looked almost as though she were trying her best to catch it before it fell. Although she seemed well within earshot, for some reason - maybe it was because of the excitement, or the blanket of snow on the ground - Elizabeth didn't appear to hear us at all. Neither her father nor I could stop the inevitable tragedy about to unfold before our widened eyes and pounding hearts.

"Elizabeth, wait! Wait!" I cried out as loud as I could, as both her father and I ran after the little girl who had become swept up in the adventure. By now she was too far ahead for either of us to snatch her back away from the icy draw of the frozen lake. Elizabeth barreled forward, heedless of her surroundings, and onto the thin blanket of snow covering the surface of the lake. Her momentum had allowed her to continue forward, and because she was a delicate girl, the thin ice supported her weight much to my amazement.

The dead goose which was somehow now taunting her came to rest silently above the deepest part of the lake. It seemed to target its destination purposefully as it was calling to Elizabeth come what may. Eerily, it was akin to witnessing a fragile moth being drawn to a flame and waiting for it to catch fire and burn. I could not avert my eyes no matter how much I wanted to. In hindsight, I wish I had just closed them and offered a prayer instead, but I admit I did no such thing. I just stood there and watched. There are some things a person should never see.

"Stop Elizabeth, come back! You're on the lake!" Her father bellowed a blast that reverberated so great I can still hear it now. His frantic voice disturbed the enveloping quietness that seemed to be mocking him as he pursued her in horror. The snow covering the ice was melting toward the deeper water, and that realization awakened Elizabeth from her frenzy and stopped her dead in her tracks. Her weight was enough to break through the ice - she dropped out of sight in an instant - disappearing from view beneath the surface of the freezing cold water. I screamed as her father ran out headlong onto the ice, but he didn't make it more than a few steps before crashing through it and into the water. I imagined the icy cold fingers of death pulling him down deeper as he struggled. I was in a state of shock as I watched him begin to swim beneath the ice, disappearing from sight just as his daughter had done. I stood there stunned and helpless, my mouth gaping, and looked on silently from the shore with a flood of tears streaming down my face. I find that it is too difficult for me to recount every horrible thing that happened - save to say just this - neither Elizabeth nor her father survived the day.

From that day forward, until many years later when my friend Jacob Marley visited me from beyond the grave, I harbored ill feelings toward Christmas as you well know. Little Tiny Tim, who reminded me often of my friend Peter Miller, gave me new hope and was the one who restored my faith in the possibilities of things hoped for. That story you already know, this detail, however, you do not. I share it with you now for the first time.

I had designated in my will that my good friend Bob Cratchit would personally ensure I was buried with a silver crown. I informed him of that request by way of a letter that was to be opened upon my death. My dying wish was that the silver crown which was locked in a box and stored in my old oak bureau would be retrieved and placed inside my casket with my body. That coin was the very same one Peter Miller's father had given to him the previous year during their first hunt together.

I have sensed that Elizabeth Miller sometimes visits my gravesite because her spirit is trapped in some netherworld, just as Jacob Marley's once was.

Something tells me that she still covets the silver crown; despite the fact that it was her strong desire for it which caused her untimely death. I feel even now that perhaps she blames me for the tragedy which claimed the life of her beloved father all those many years ago. Elizabeth haunts me even still in my memory of that day, but it was the loss of her life at such an early age that turned my stomach at the thought of Christmas when I was just an impressionable boy.

Six days after the accident, the worst possible thing I could have ever imagined happened. My friend Peter was found by his mother, hanging from a beam inside his barn. I felt as though he was more of a brother than a friend, but he decided to keep his grief to himself nonetheless. Perhaps deep down inside he too believed that I should have done something more to prevent what happened. My transformation allowed me the ability to forgive myself for my part in his misguided departure from earth. Had I known his secret intentions, I know that we would have reached some compromise concerning his life. We both would have lived long prosperous lives, continuing our friendship for many years if only I had the chance to talk with him before he departed.

After Peter's death, just one day shy of a fortnight, his mother bestowed to me the silver crown that he had gotten from his father one year prior. She was convinced that he would have wanted me to have it. That is the coin my body is now buried with. At my funeral, Bob Cratchit kindly slipped it into my breast pocket, to keep it close to my heart forever.

Hold steadfast and prepare yourselves now, for you are about to peer through ethereal eyes, and into the future. You may be shocked, confused, and frightened by what you have been chosen to see. However, remember that this is only a possible shadow of things to come. For a brief moment or two, I will surrender myself to another spectre, and my eyes will become as his in this bizarre assignation of time and space. Your journey ahead in time begins now.

Inhabitants of the vestige of the fabric of space, behind that veil - I am Chronos - father of time. Do not attempt to exit the modepi! For your own safety be advised that there is no way to return once the tour has begun. The vehicle embarks now, and I shall show you portents of a future, of a world that is to come. Its shape and form flow from the business that flourishes along perpetually industrious Avenue E. We have departed the present. Do not attempt to disembark the modepi until you hear the sound of the exit bell.

The current consensus here is that the metaphylum which causes, creates, and cultivates scientism is no longer considered to be imagined but a stark reality. Wait! I apologize. I failed to mention that much of this information has been classified for eons, and it may seem to come at you in waves, or in a flash. Let me slow down the process so as not to blind your eyes as they are opened to the nature of the previously invisible. The invisible - like the surface of a frozen lake hidden beneath a blanket of freshly fallen snow - is a circumstance which can prove to be irrefutably dangerous when ignored.

Metaphylum are those invisible agents who collectively work to promote and advocate or classify the geocentric experience. They are ever-present and influence billions of people on earth every day. I personally have been engaged for many millennia in the advancement of self-edification, and that is why I am here today guiding you in your discovery, your fact-finding mission. I shall begin again with just a bit more consideration for your perspective because the view from here is dramatically different from where you are at present.

Peer through this portal with me and see with your own eyes. Observe a unilaterally subsidized research laboratory staffed by ordinary people and metaphylum alike. What you are witnessing has already begun in the geocentric universe; it is the development of sentient bio-genetic life. Scientifically, there are those attempting to determine the cause of some very bizarre behaviors and unexplained phenomena. There are cases which I have been involved in that I must admit were very brilliantly executed. Watch as the world at large relies on the scientific realm to screen the facts and purport what is real. Enamored with technical jargon and sophisticated nomenclature scientism is very much appreciated by my associates and me. It is useful to us because of its effectiveness as a coded re-education process. We now have come to realize that many human beings have converted to scientism as a basis for the creation and explanation of all things in existence.

Turn your eyes toward the surface of your planet below, witness the flash of destruction and the decimation of the landscape. This vision is the end of the age, the termination of your 3rd millennium. Observe the devastation and power of my wieldy scythe. The year of this cataclysm is 2066. It ironically comes just six years beyond the prophesied date which your intuitive scientist Isaac Newton is credited for calculating. As the annus calamitosus of 166 fundamentally reduced the Roman Empire to ruins, and as the Great Fire of

London and the Great Plague in 1666 brought that kingdom to its knees - 2066 will be the end of all things now known to the geocentric realm of mankind! Perhaps that information has long been hidden in the number of books of the Bible known as the Canon of Divine Revelation; that number is 66.

Scientism will become the veil that causes the shadows and brings the darkness, ultimately blanketing your planet, despite its impressive conjecture and research into the realm of which I claim eminent domain. It will inadvertently unleash the destruction and devastation which all of you have only captured a glimpse of here. The development of artificial intelligence, paired with the diversion from the simplicities of life such as sharing the milk of human kindness, will become the Ignorance and Want of future days for the Earth and all of its inhabitants. These images are reflected in the mirrors of my ethereal eyes. Gaze deeply into them, peer into my soul, and you will become mesmerized. I am Chronos, lord of the bustling Avenue E, and the edification of the geocentric realm. Follow my path, I await your arrival. Honor me as does the Dirge of My Reverence!

I am, say I, and all shall heed my thundering cry,

Just as mountains rumble into rubble, and rivers run dry

Swinging the scythe with henchman's hand, at my command

As you comply - for I watch the world with my tearless cosmic eye

Demanding the hourglass spin, as dirges chime untimely goodbyes

Your hymns and rhymes do pantomime, but alas never disguise

Resonate and revelate rhetorically sublime

And yet your eyes reflect - but cannot define

Behind your refined mind and infinite repose; your mortality shows

Day after day trepidation grows while resolutely clinging -

To the caress, of the red, red rose…

But this vision, beauty as an intervention - capturing your attention,

Enamels the frown on the face of my ticking clock

Whose race mocks you - day by day - tick tock

Its hands distracting, trying to block your view by beckoning you

Yet unlocking the fear of my reckoning,

Hoping the day may disappear...

Dry your tears when an infant and rainbow appears-

A stormy sky clears - embrace your years...

Remembering how the sunset gleams and then gives way,

Moonbeams shimmer and shine, and pine, to defy the day

I say, enjoy the fragrance of each flower, every rose

In life's bountiful bouquet - hour by hour, and day by day...

And so it goes, drink deeply from the well -

And ignore the sound of the chiming bell,

The chiming bell...

Awaken from the spell cast upon you by Chronos; for the bell has rung while you became transfixed by his subtle plea for your submission and obedience. It is I once again, the invisible embodiment of Scrooge, your host. Now you must witness the foreshadowing of another world. The paradox of the future you have just been horrified by is all but behind you now. We must make haste and press onward to tour Tabula Rasa Road, passing post-2066, manifestations yet unseen eagerly await us there. Once again, for a mere moment or two, I will surrender myself to another, and you will see your future through his eyes in this heralded assignation of space, and time. He speaks to you now.

I have been made aware that many of you recently toured Avenue E in the modepi that floats like a bubble in the prevailing wind. Summoned here to guide you to a different destination, where the fare is free, I heed my master's call. The price of passage on the journey along Avenue E follows a course which spans across the chasm of time and space, and that cost is your attention. Within the fleeting geocentric realm you just observed, its manifestations are the only reward it offers. As you just witnessed, its approaching end is coming soon. Have you assimilated here that Chronos is a master of casting spells, so that time passes in the blink of an eye? Beware of such folly for there are greater things to behold in this kingdom.

Breathe in the fresh air along Tabula Rasa Rd. While I pilot the modepi, you may roam about as you wish, so relax and enjoy the scenery. The view from here is exquisite as it passes through a world imagined by many. It is a world where scientism does not exist, there are no weapons to wield, and no countries to create derision. There is neither hate nor destruction here. Peace is the key to the uniqueness and beauty of this eternal realm.

If you would kindly fix your gaze at the world below, you will observe that here there is no pollution, no poverty or squalor, and beauty prevails as the planet itself has undergone its own trans-mutational, transformative transition. The single most significant shift is the fact that all of the inhabitants of Avenue E have vacated this reality entirely by a vehicle of their own volition. Dispersion has occurred as a result of their conditionally limited bubble enclosure bursting, having ever only existed here as an illusion. For time itself is merely an illusion modeled within the bubble known as the third dimension. That is the secret heart of the geocentric realm where the limitations of only three dimensions and five senses require only a fraction of the genetic components to be actively engaged.

On this neo-planet, a world after 2066, all of the genetic composition is energized through the trans-mutational process. This world, once established as a post-Edenic paradise, resonates with a radiance that can only be perceived by the regenerated genetic material. This trans-mutational process represents not only a barrier to shield its existence from those confined within the aforementioned bubble, but it simultaneously opens new portals of experience and wonder. This radiance is a frequency undetectable by those inhabitants of Avenue E because their attention is focused so intently elsewhere - deep within the edification process of existence. Just as the world is the prize for the geocentric realm, the genetic awakening of DNA is the reward for resisting the temptations of Chronos and the metaphylum he controls so effectively.

There are those who claim that Chronos is gracious and as such willingly adhere to his ways which they alone are privy to, yet he never reveals which heading the direction of the Avenue on which he operates leads. The goal he so enthusiastically facilitates as he conducts such nefarious business in so many darkened corners is his eternal curse. I have shared this with you because you have chosen a better path, a path known as the Tabula Rasa Rd. Wise is your choice - from the sound of my voice - to the words I have said. Awaken now Joseph, awaken now!

"It is still dark and so early yet. Was I dreaming? Who are you? Wait! I have seen you before. What has happened, and why did you reveal those visions to me?"

"I am the angel sent to guide and protect you. You must escort your wife and unborn child to Bethlehem, for the time has come. Your child will become the master of Chronos, and now Joseph you know the magnificence of whom you were chosen to be guardian over. Embrace the magnitude of his birth."

I, Ebenezer Scrooge, impart this knowledge of the Christmas Spirit for the benefit of all mankind. It was revealed to me in a conversation with Joseph himself when once our paths met on this infinite plane of existence. As he described what he had been shown in a vision by the angel who spoke to him, I have now shared it with you. I shall depart your world one last time. This time my exit is forever, farewell to you all. As my good friend Tiny Tim said all those years ago, "God bless us, everyone."